THE USBORNE INTERNET-LINKED

FIRST THOUSAND WORDS

IN ITALIAN

With Internet-linked pronunciation guide

Heather Amery

Illustrated by Stephen Cartwright

Edited by Nicole Irving and Mairi Mackinnon
Designed by Andy Griffin

Italian language consultant: Giovanna Iannaco

About Usborne Quicklinks

To access the Usborne Quicklinks Web site for this book, go to
www.usborne-quicklinks.com
and enter the keywords "1000 italian". There you can:

- listen to the first thousand words in Italian, read by a native Italian speaker
- print out some Italian picture puzzles for free
- find links to other useful Web sites about Italy and the Italian language

Listening to the words

To hear the words in this book, you will need your Web browser
(e.g. Internet Explorer or Netscape Navigator) and a program that lets you play sound
(such as RealPlayer® or Windows® Media Player). These programs are free and, if you
don't already have one of them, you can download them from Usborne Quicklinks.
Your computer also needs a sound card but most
computers already have one of these.

Note for parents and guardians

Please ensure that your children read and follow the Internet safety
guidelines displayed on the Usborne Quicklinks Web site.

The links in Usborne Quicklinks are regularly reviewed and updated.
However, the content of a Web site may change at any time and Usborne Publishing
is not responsible for the content on any Web site other than its own. We recommend
that children are supervised while on the Internet, that they do not use
Internet Chat Rooms, and that you use Internet filtering software to block
unsuitable material. For more information, see the **Net Help**
area on the Usborne Quicklinks Web site.

On every double page with pictures,
there is a little yellow duck to look for.
Can you find it?

About this book

This is a great book for anyone starting to learn Italian. You'll find it easy to learn new words by looking at the small, labeled pictures. Then you can practice the words by talking about the large central pictures. This book also has its own Usborne Quicklinks Web site where you can listen to all the Italian words, print out Italian picture puzzles, and follow links to some other fun and useful Web sites.

Masculine and feminine words

When you look at Italian words for things such as "chair" or "man", you will see that they have **il**, **lo**, **la** or **l'** in front of them. This is because all Italian words for things and people are either masculine or feminine. **Il** or **lo** are the words for "the" in front of a masculine word and **la** is "the" in front of a feminine word. You use **l'** in front of words that begin with "a", "e", "i", "o" or "u". In front of the words that are plural (more than one, such as "chairs" or "men"), the Italian word for "the" is **i** or **gli** for masculine words, and **le** for feminine words.

All the labels in this book show words for things with **il**, **lo**, **la**, **l'**, **i**, **gli** or **le**. Always learn them with this little word.

Looking at Italian words

A few Italian words have an accent on the last letter of the word. This is a sign written over the letter, and means that the last part of the word is stressed when it is spoken.

Saying Italian words

The best way to learn how to say Italian words is to listen to an Italian speaker and repeat what you hear. You can listen to all the words in this book on the Usborne Quicklinks Web site. For more information on how to do this, see the page on the left. At the back of this book, there is also a word list with an easy pronunciation guide for each Italian word.

A computer is not essential

If you don't have access to the Internet, don't worry. This book is a complete and excellent Italian word book on its own.

A casa

la vasca

il sapone

il rubinetto

la carta igienica

lo spazzolino

l'acqua

il water

la spugna

il lavandino

la doccia

il letto

Il bagno

Il soggiorno

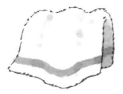
l'asciugamano

il dentifricio

la radio

il cuscino

il Compact Disc

la moquette

il divano

la sedia

il piumone

il pettine

il lenzuolo

il tappeto

l'armadio

La camera da letto

il guanciale

il cassettone

lo specchio

la spazzola

L'ingresso

la lampada

i poster

l'attaccapanni

il telefono

il radiatore

la videocassetta

il giornale

il tavolino

le lettere

le scale

5

La cucina

il frigorifero

i bicchieri

l'orologio

lo sgabello

i cucchiaini

l'interruttore

il detersivo

la chiave

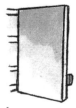
la porta

il lavello

l'aspirapolvere

le pentole

le forchette

il grembiule

l'asse da stiro

la spazzatura

6

il bollitore

 i coltelli

 lo spazzolone

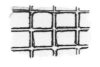 lo straccio

le mattonelle

la scopa

 la lavatrice

 la paletta

il cassetto

i piattini

la padella

la cucina

 i mestoli

 i piatti

 il ferro da stiro

 l'armadietto

 l'asciugatoio

 le tazze

 i fiammiferi

 la spazzola

 le scodelle

7

Il giardino

la carriola

l'alveare

la chiocciola

i mattoni

il piccione

la vanga

la coccinella

la pattumiera

i semi

il casotto

l'annaffiatoio

il verme

i fiori

l'annaffiatore

la zappa

la vespa

l'ape

la paletta

l'osso

la siepe

il forcone

il tosaerba

il sentiero

le foglie

l'albero

il fumo

il bruco

il rastrello

il nido

i ramoscelli

l'erba

la carrozzina

la scala

il falò

il tubo di gomma

la serra

Il laboratorio

le viti

la morsa

la carta vetrata

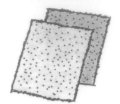
il trapano

la scala

la sega

la segatura

il calendario

la cassetta
degli arnesi

il cacciavite

l'asse

i trucioli

il temperino

10

le bullette

il ragno

i bulloni

i dadi

la ragnatela

la botte

la mosca

l'ascia

il metro

il martello

la lima

la vernice

la pialla

il legno

i chiodi

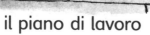
il piano di lavoro

i barattoli

La strada

il negozio

il buco

il bar

l'ambulanza

il marciapiede

l'antenna

il comignolo

il tetto

la scavatrice

l'autobus

l'albergo

l'uomo

la macchina della polizia

le condutture

il martello pneumatico

la scuola

il campo giochi

il taxi

le strisce pedonali

la fabbrica

il camion

il semaforo

il cinema

il furgone

lo schiacciasassi

il rimorchio

la casa

il mercato

gli scalini

la motocicletta

la bicicletta

l'autopompa

il vigile urbano

la macchina

la donna

il lampione

il palazzo

13

il trenino

i dadi

il flauto dolce

il robot

i tamburi

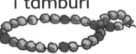
la collana

la macchina
fotografica

le perline

le bambole

la chitarra

l'anello

la casa
delle bambole

I giocattoli

l'armonica

il fischietto

le
costruzioni

il castello

il sottomarino

la tromba

le frecce

l'arco

il paracadute

la barca

i colori per
il viso

lo
schiacciasassi

le maschere

la macchina
da corsa

il cavallo a dondolo

il salvadanaio

le biglie

le marionette

il pianoforte

gli astronauti

la gru

la plastilina

il fucile

i soldatini

gli acquarelli

il razzo

le altalene

la buca di sabbia

il picnic

l'aquilone

il gelato

il cane

il cancello

il sentiero

la rana

lo scivolo

Il parco

la panchina

i girini

il lago

i rollerblades

il cespuglio

 il bebè

 lo skateboard

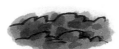 la terra

 il passeggino

 l'altalena a bilico

 i bambini

 il triciclo

 gli uccelli

 la cancellata

 la palla

 la barca

 lo spago

 la pozzanghera

 gli anatroccoli

 la corda per saltare

 gli alberi

l'aiuola

i cigni

il guinzaglio

le anatre

Lo zoo

le ali

l'aquila

l'ippopotamo

il panda

le zampe

il pipistrello

il gorilla

il canguro

la scimmia

l'iceberg

il pinguino

la coda

il lupo

il coccodrillo

l'orso

le piume

il pellicano

lo struzzo

il delfino

il leone

i leoncini

la giraffa

le corna

il cervo

il dromedario

la foca

l'orso polare

la tartaruga

l'elefante

la proboscide

il rinoceronte

il bisonte

il castoro

il serpente

la zebra

la capra

lo squalo

la balena

la tigre

il leopardo

19

I trasporti

i binari

il locomotore

i respingenti

i vagoni

il macchinista

il treno merci

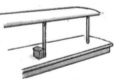
la pensilina

il controllore

la valigia

la biglietteria automatica

l'elicottero

La stazione ferroviaria

La stazione di servizio

i segnali

lo zaino

i fari

il motore

la ruota

la batteria

l'aereo

l'hostess

la pista di atterraggio

la torre di controllo

L'aeroporto

lo steward

il pilota

l'autolavaggio

il portabagagli

la benzina

il carro attrezzi

AUTOLAVAGGIO

l'autocisterna

la chiave inglese

il pneumatico

il cofano

l'olio

il distributore di benzina

il mulino a vento

La campagna

la montagna

la mongolfiera

la farfalla

la lucertola

le pietre

la volpe

il ruscello

il cartello
stradale

il riccio

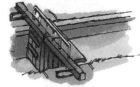

la chiusa

lo scoiattolo   la foresta

il tasso

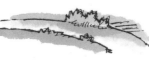

il fiume

la strada

le tende

il canale

i ceppi

il villaggio

la falena

il ponte

la chiatta

la cascata

il gufo

la galleria

i volpacchiotti

la talpa

il pescatore

i massi

il rospo

il treno

la roulotte

la collina

La fattoria

il mucchio di fieno

il cane pastore

le anatre

gli agnelli

lo stagno

i pulcini

il fienile

il porcile

il toro

gli anatroccoli

il pollaio

il trattore

il gallo

il trattore

le oche

l'autocisterna

il capannone

il fango

il carretto

24

l'agricoltore

il campo

le galline

il vitello

la staccionata

la sella

la stalla

la mucca

l'aratro

il frutteto

la scuderia

i maialini

la pastorella

i tacchini

lo spaventapasseri

la casa colonica

il fieno

le pecore

le balle di paglia

il cavallo

i maiali

la barca a vela

Al mare

la conchiglia

il mare

il remo

il faro

la paletta

il secchiello

la stella marina

il castello
di sabbia

l'ombrellone

la bandiera

il marinaio

il granchio

il gabbiano   l'isola

il motoscafo   lo sci nautico

le onde

il cappello da sole

la scogliera

la nave

la canoa

la fune

i ciottoli

le alghe

la rete

la pagaia

il peschereccio

le pinne

l'asino

il pesce

la sedia a sdraio

il costume da bagno

la petroliera

la spiaggia

la barca a remi

A scuola

le forbici

2 + 2 = 4
3 + 2 = 5

le addizioni

la gomma

il righello

le fotografie

i pennarelli

le puntine
da disegno

i colori

il bambino

il righello

la matita

la lavagna

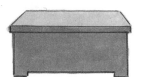

il banco

i libri

la penna

la colla

i gessetti

il disegno

28

il cestino della carta

l'insegnante

la scatola

la carta geografica

il pennello

il soffitto

la parete

il pavimento

il quaderno

l'alfabeto

la spilla

l'acquario

la carta

l'avvolgibile

il cavalletto

la maniglia della porta

la pianta

il mappamondo

la bambina

i pastelli

la lampada

l'infermiere

il cotone idrofilo

la medicina

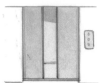
l'ascensore

la vestaglia

le grucce

le pillole

il vassoio

l'orologio

il termometro

la tenda

L'ospedale

l'orsacchiotto

la mela

il gesso

la fascia

la sedia a rotelle

il puzzle

la dottoressa

la siring(a)

Dal dottore

le pantofole

il computer

il cerotto

la banana

l'uva

il cestino

i giocattoli

la pera

le cartoline

il pannolino

il bastone

il televisore

la camicia da notte

il pigiama

l'arancia

i fazzoletti di carta

il fumetto

la sala d'aspetto

31

La festa

il palloncino

la cioccolata

la caramella

la finestra

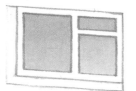

i fuochi d'artificio

il nastro

la torta

i regali

la cannuccia   la candela

le decorazioni di carta

i giocattoli

il mandarino

 il salame

 la musicassetta

 la salsiccia

 le patatine

 i costumi

 la ciliegia

 il succo di frutta

 il lampone

 la fragola

 la lampadina

 il panino

 il burro

 il biscotto

 il formaggio

 il pane

 la tovaglia

33

Il negozio

il pompelmo

la carota

il cavolfiore

il porro

il fungo

il cetriolo

il limone

il sedano

l'albicocca

il melone

la borsa della spesa

FORMAGGI

FRUTTA E VERDURA

la cipolla

il cavolo

la pesca

la lattuga

i piselli

il pomodoro

34

le uova

 la susina

 la farina

 la bilancia

 i barattoli

 la carne

 l'ananas

 lo yogurt

 il cestino

 le bottiglie

 la borsa

 il borsellino

 i soldi

 il cibo in scatola

 il carrello

 le patate

gli spinaci

i fagiolini

 la cassa

la zucca

35

I pasti

la colazione

il pranzo

il caffè

l'uovo sodo

l'uovo fritto

il pane tostato

la marmellata

la panna

il latte

i cereali

la cioccolata calda

lo zucchero

il tè

il miele

il sale

il pepe

la teiera

le frittelle

i panini

36

la cena

il prosciutto

la minestra

la frittata

le bacchette

l'insalata

l'hamburger

il pollo

il riso

il ketchup

gli spaghetti

il purè

la pizza

le patatine fritte

i dolci

37

Me stesso

la testa

i capelli

il viso

le sopracciglia

l'occhio

il naso

la guancia

la bocca

le labbra

il braccio

il gomito

la pancia

i denti

la lingua

il mento

le orecchie

il collo

le spalle

le dita dei piedi

il piede

la gamba

il ginocchio

il torace

la schiena

il sedere

la mano

il pollice

le dita della mano

I vestiti

 i calzini

 le mutande

 la canottiera

 i pantaloni

 i jeans

 la maglietta

 la gonna

 la camicia

 la cravatta

 i pantaloncini

 la calzamaglia

 il vestito

 il maglione

 la felpa

 il cardigan

 la sciarpa

 il fazzoletto

 le scarpe da ginnastica

 le scarpe

 i sandali

 gli stivali di gomma

 i guanti

 le tasche

 la cintura

 la fibbia

 la cerniera lampo

 i lacci per le scarpe

 i bottoni

le asole

 le tasche

 il cappotto

 il giubbotto

 il berretto

 il cappello

I mestieri

il cuoco

i ballerini

l'attore   l'attrice

i cantanti

l'astronauta

il macellaio

i poliziotti

il falegname

il pompiere

l'artista

il giudice

i méccanici

40

il parrucchiere

la camionista

il conducente di autobus

il cameriere   la cameriera

il postino

la dentista

il subacqueo

l'imbianchino

la fornaia

La famiglia

la zia   lo zio

il nonno

il figlio   la figlia   la madre   il padre
il fratello   la sorella   la moglie   il marito   il cugino   la nonna

Le azioni

sorridere

ridere

piangere

pensare

ascoltare

acchiappare

lanciare

rompere

dipingere

scrivere

spaccare

tagliare

mangiare

parlare

scavare

portare

bere

fare

saltare

ballare

lavarsi

lavorare a maglia

camminare a carponi

giocare

guardare

arrampicarsi

fare a botte

dormire

prendere

cucire

saltare la corda

aspettare

cucinare

nascondersi

leggere

comprare

spingere

cantare

soffiare

tirare

spazzare

raccogliere

cadere

camminare

correre

stare seduti

43

I contrari

buono

cattivo

lontano

vicino

in cima

in fondo

freddo

caldo

bagnato

asciutto

sporco

pulito

sopra

sotto

grasso

magro

aperto

chiuso

piccolo

grande

pochi

molti

primo

ultimo

sinistra

44

fuori

dentro

facile

difficile

vuoto

pieno

morbido

duro

davanti

alto

lento

veloce

dietro

basso

lungo

corto

morto

vivo

scuro

chiaro

vecchio

su

destra

nuovo

giù

I giorni

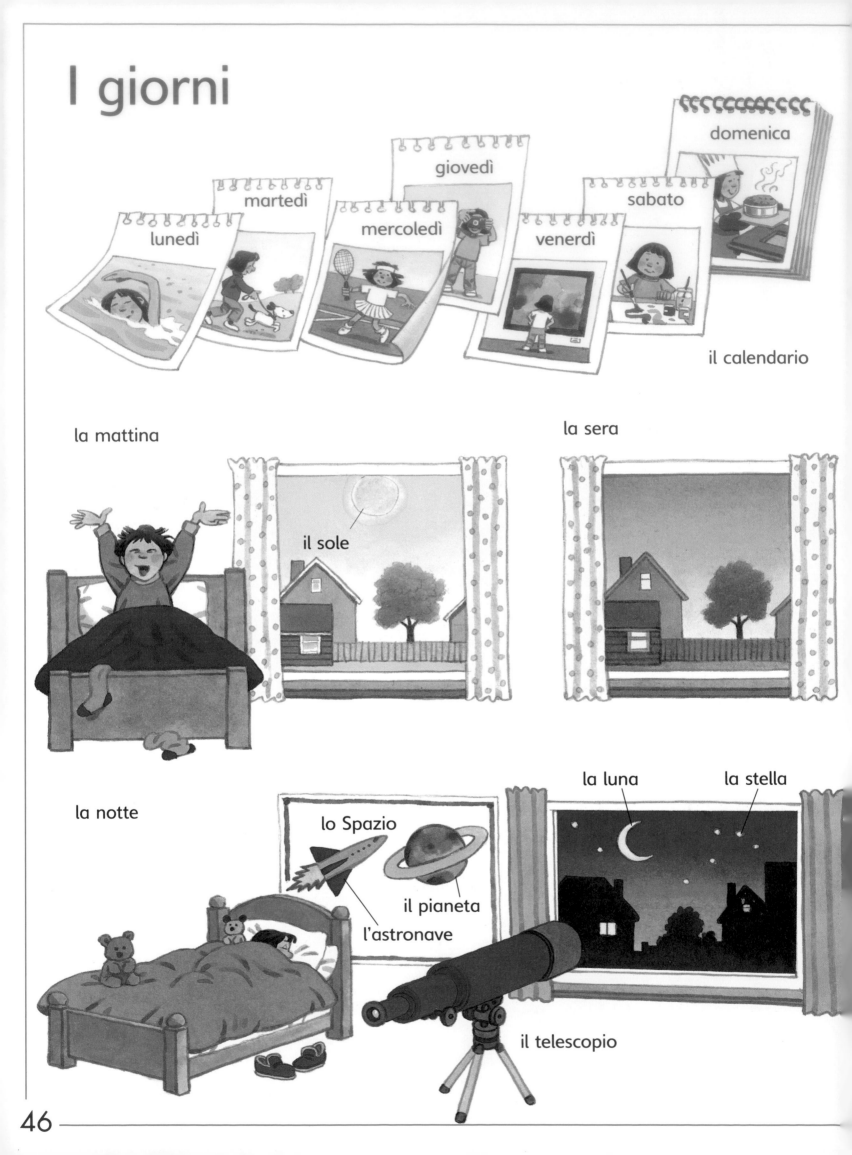

lunedì
martedì
mercoledì
giovedì
venerdì
sabato
domenica

il calendario

la mattina

la sera

il sole

la notte

lo Spazio

il pianeta

l'astronave

la luna

la stella

il telescopio

46

Giorni speciali

il compleanno

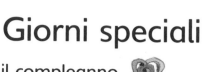

le candeline

il biglietto
di auguri

il regalo

la torta

la vacanza

il matrimonio

la damigella
d'onore

la sposa

lo sposo

la macchina
fotografica

il fotografo

Natale

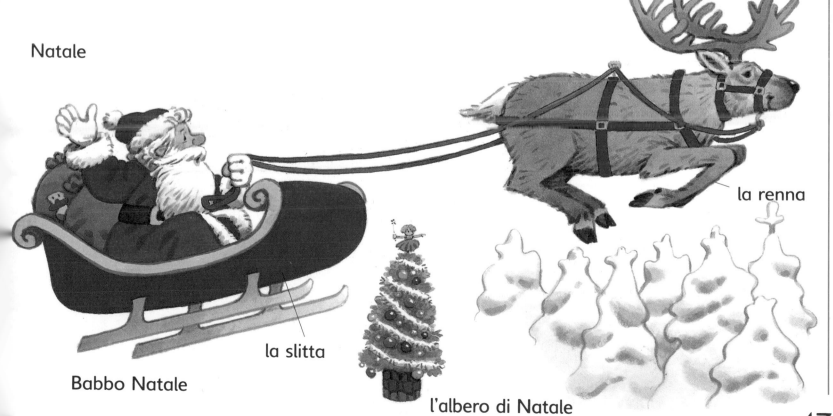

la renna

la slitta

Babbo Natale

l'albero di Natale

47

Il tempo

l'ombrello

il sole

le nuvole

il cielo

la pioggia

il lampo

la nebbia

la neve

la rugiada

il vento

la foschia

la brina

l'arcobaleno

Le stagioni

la primavera

l'estate

l'autunno

l'inverno

Gli animali domestici

il criceto

il veterinario

la cuccia

il porcellino d'India

il cagnolino

il cane

il pappagallino

il pappagallo

il becco

il cibo

il canarino

il coniglio

la gabbia

il gatto

la cesta

il topolino

il gattino

il latte

i pesci rossi

49

Lo sport

il canottaggio

lo snowboard

la vela

il windsurf

la pallacanestro

il cricket

il karatè

la racchetta

la mazza

il tennis

il football americano

la ginnastica artistica

la palla

la danza

il baseball

la pesca

la canna da pesca

l'esca

il rugby

i tuffi

la piscina

il nuoto

la corsa campestre

il bersaglio

il tiro con l'arco

il volo libero

il casco

il jogging

il ciclismo

l'alpinismo

il judo

il cavallo

il pony

l'armadietto

il calcio

lo spogliatoio

l'equitazione

il badminton

i pattini

il ping-pong

il pattinaggio su ghiaccio

i bastoncini da sci

la seggiovia

gli sci

lo sci

il sumo

I colori

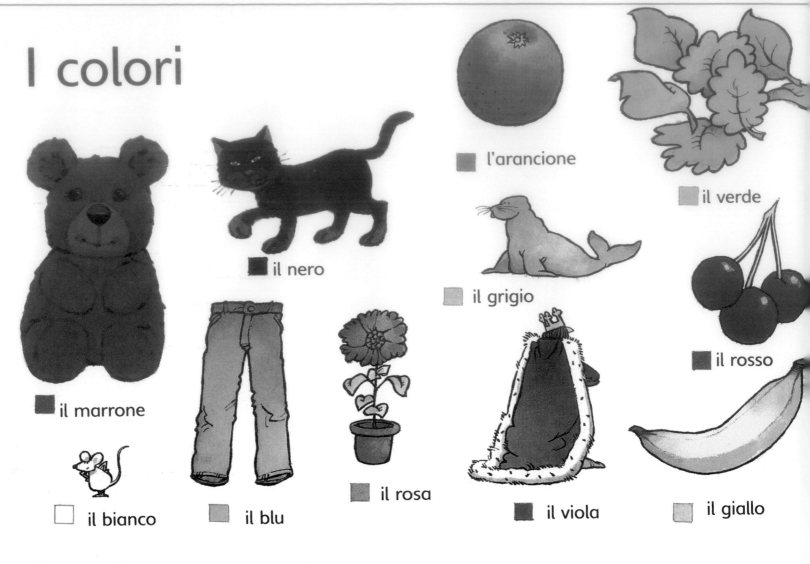

l'arancione

il verde

il nero

il grigio

il rosso

il marrone

il rosa

il viola

il giallo

il bianco

il blu

Le forme

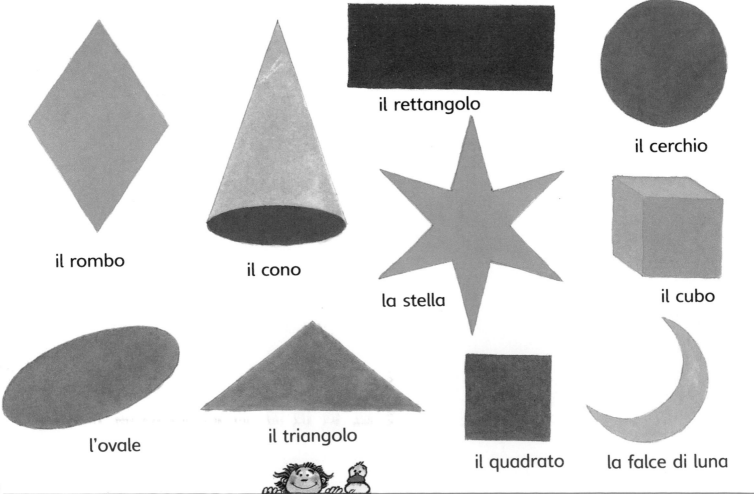

il rettangolo

il cerchio

il rombo

il cono

la stella

il cubo

l'ovale

il triangolo

il quadrato

la falce di luna

I numeri

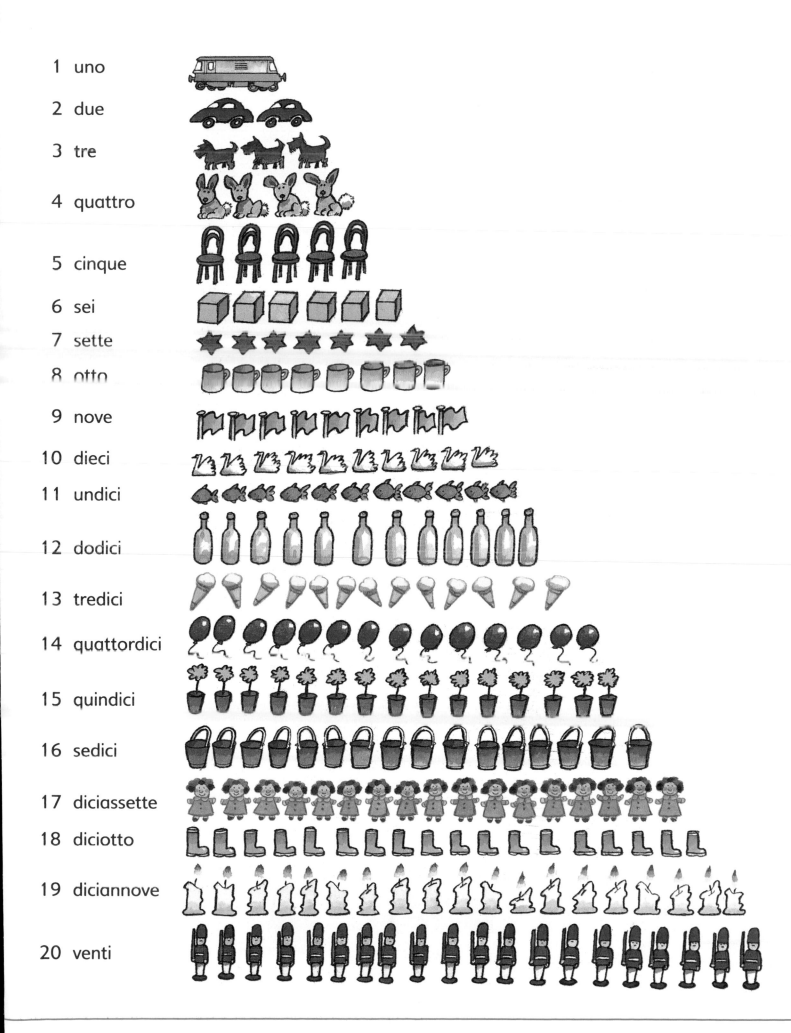

1 uno
2 due
3 tre
4 quattro
5 cinque
6 sei
7 sette
8 otto
9 nove
10 dieci
11 undici
12 dodici
13 tredici
14 quattordici
15 quindici
16 sedici
17 diciassette
18 diciotto
19 diciannove
20 venti

Il luna park

la giostra

il tappetino

lo scivolo

la ruota

il trenino dei fantasmi

il pop-corn

il tiro al
cerchietto

le montagne russe

il tiro a segno

l'autoscontro

lo zucchero filato

Il circo

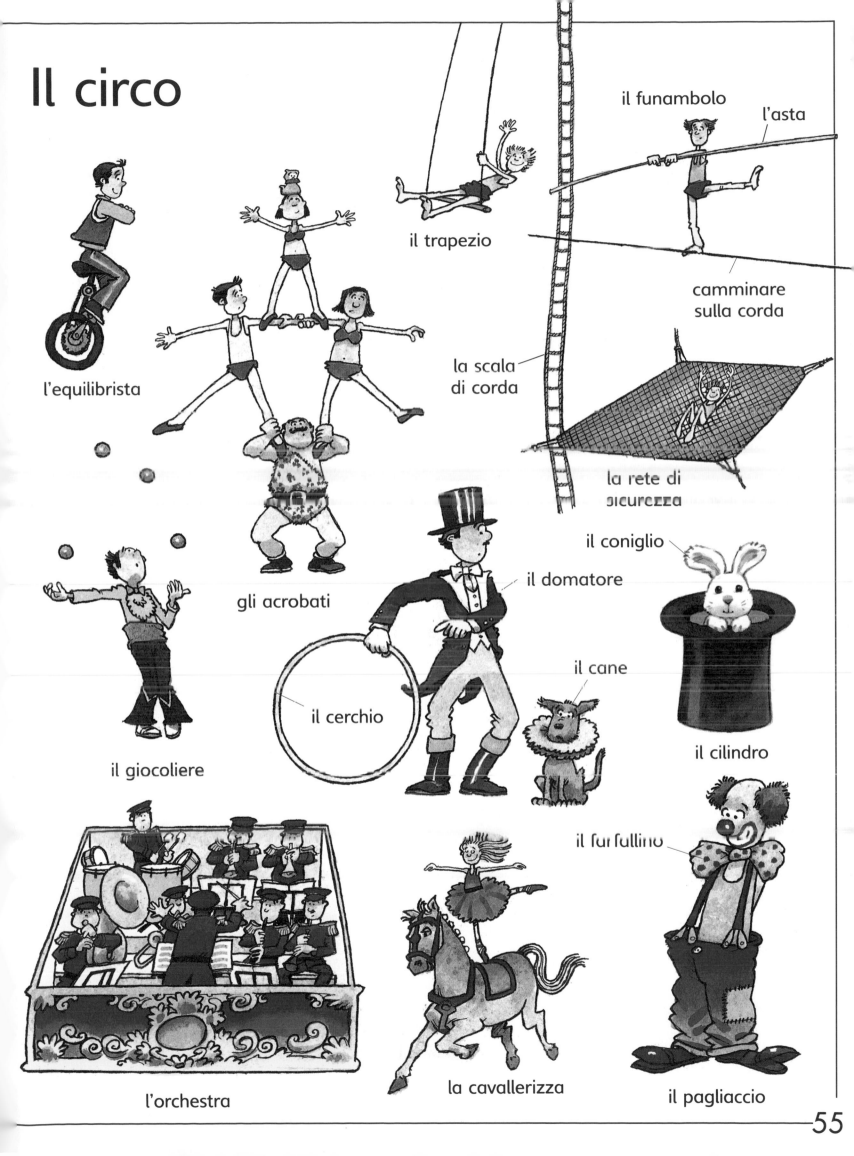

il funambolo

l'asta

il trapezio

camminare sulla corda

l'equilibrista

la scala di corda

la rete di sicurezza

il coniglio

il domatore

gli acrobati

il cane

il cerchio

il cilindro

il giocoliere

il farfallino

l'orchestra

la cavallerizza

il pagliaccio

55

Word list

In this list you can find all the Italian words in this book. They are listed in alphabetical order. Next to each one, you can see its pronunciation (how to say it) in letters *like this*, and then its English translation.

Remember that Italian nouns (words for things) are either masculine or feminine (see page 3). In the list, each one has **il**, **lo**, **la**, **l'**, **i**, **gli** or **le** in front of it. These all mean "the". The words with **il** or **lo** are masculine, those with **la** are feminine. Italian nouns that begin with "a", "e", "i", "o" or "u" have **l'** in front of them. After the word you will see **(m)** or **(f)** to show whether it is masculine or feminine.

Plural nouns (a noun is plural if you are talking about more than one, for example "cats") have **i** or **gli** in front if they are masculine, or **le** if they are feminine.

About Italian pronunciation
Read the pronunciation as if it were an English word, but try to remember the following points about how Italian words are said:

All the letters in an Italian word are sounded, except 'h';
Double letters, like 'll' or 'nn', sound a little longer than usual;

c before *e* or *i* is pronounced *ch*;

ch before *e* or *i* is pronounced *k*;

gh before *e* or *i* is pronounced *g* as in *get*;

sc before *e* or *i* is pronounced *sh*;

z is pronounced *ts*.

Most Italian words have a part that you stress, or say louder (like the "day" part of the English word "today"). So you know which part of each word you should stress, it is shown in letters ***like this***, in the pronunciation guide;

In the guide, *ay* is like the *a* in date;

o is like the *o* in *hot*;

ow is like the *ow* in *cow*;

g is always like the *g* in *get*;

ly is like the *lli* in *million*;

ny is like the *ni* in *onion*;

ye is always like the *ye* in *yet*.

A

Italian	Pronunciation	English
acchiappare	*akkyapparay*	to catch
l'acqua (f)	*lakwa*	water
gli acquarelli	*lyee akwarellee*	paints
l'acquario (m)	*lakwaryo*	aquarium
gli acrobati	*lyee akrobatee*	acrobats
le addizioni	*lay addeetsyonee*	sums
l'aereo (m)	*la-ayrayo*	airplane
l'aeroporto (m)	*la-ayroporto*	airport
gli agnelli	*lyee anyellee*	lambs
l'agricoltore	*lagreekoltoray*	farmer
l'aiuola (f)	*la-yuola*	flower bed
l'albergo (m)	*lalbairgo*	hotel
gli alberi	*lyee albairee*	trees
l'albero (m)	*lalbairo*	tree
l'albero (m) di Natale	*lalbairo dee natalay*	Christmas tree
l'albicocca (f)	*lalbeekokka*	apricot
l'alfabeto (m)	*lalfabayto*	alphabet
le alghe	*lay algay*	seaweed
le ali	*lay alee*	wings
l'alpinismo (m)	*lalpeeneezmo*	climbing
l'altalena (f) a bilico	*laltalayna a beeleeko*	seesaw
le altalene	*lay altalaynay*	swings
alto	*alto*	high
l'alveare (m)	*lalvayaray*	beehive
l'ambulanza (f)	*lamboolantsa*	ambulance
l'ananas (m)	*lananass*	pineapple
le anatre	*lay anatray*	ducks
gli anatroccoli	*lyee anatrokkolee*	ducklings
l'anello (m)	*lanello*	ring
gli animali domestici	*lyee aneemalee domesteechee*	pets
l'annaffiatoio (m)	*lanaffyatoyo*	watering can
l'annaffiatore (m)	*lanaffyatoray*	sprinkler
l'antenna (f)	*lantenna*	antenna
l'ape (f)	*lapay*	bee
aperto	*apairto*	open
l'aquila (f)	*lakweela*	eagle
l'aquilone (m)	*lakweelonay*	kite
l'arancia (f)	*larancha*	orange (fruit)
l'arancione (m)	*aranchonay*	orange (color)
l'aratro (m)	*laratro*	plow
l'arco (m)	*larko*	bow (and arrows)
l'arcobaleno (m)	*larkobalayno*	rainbow
l'armadietto (m)	*larmadyetto*	cupboard
l'armadio (m)	*larmadyo*	closet
l'armonica (f)	*larmoneeka*	harmonica
arrampicarsi	*arrampeekarsee*	to climb
l'artista (m/f)	*larteesta*	artist
l'ascensore (m)	*lashensoray*	lift
l'ascia (f)	*lasha*	ax
l'asciugamano (m)	*lashoogamano*	towel
l'asciugatoio (m)	*lashoogatoyo*	dish towel
asciutto	*ashootto*	dry
ascoltare	*askoltaray*	to listen
l'asino (m)	*lazeeno*	donkey
le asole	*lay azolay*	button holes
aspettare	*aspettaray*	to wait
l'aspirapolvere (m)	*laspeerapolvairay*	vacuum cleaner
l'asse (f)	*lassay*	plank
l'asse (f) da stiro	*lassay da steero*	board
l'asta (f)	*lasta*	pole
l'astronave (f)	*lastronavay*	spaceship
l'astronauta (m)	*lastronowta*	astronaut
gli astronauti	*lyee astronowtee*	astronauts, spacemen
l'attaccapanni (m)	*lattakkapannee*	coat rack
l'attore (m)	*lattoray*	actor
l'attrice (f)	*lattreechay*	actress
l'autobus (m)	*lowtoboos*	bus
l'autocisterna (f)	*lowtocheestairna*	tanker truck
l'autolavaggio (m)	*lowtolavajjo*	car wash
l'autopompa (f)	*lowtopompa*	fire truck

Italian	Pronunciation	English
l'autoscontro (m)	*lowtoskontro*	bumper cars
l'autunno (m)	*lowtoonno*	autumn
l'avvolgibile (m)	*lavvoljeebeelay*	blind
le azioni	*lay atsyonee*	actions

B

Italian	Pronunciation	English
Babbo Natale	*babbo natalay*	Santa Claus
le bacchette	*lay bakkettay*	chopsticks
il badminton	*eel badmeenton*	badminton
bagnato	*banyato*	wet
il bagno	*eel banyo*	bathroom
la balena	*la balayna*	whale
ballare	*ballaray*	to dance
le balle di paglia	*lay ballay dee palya*	straw bales
i ballerini	*ee ballaireenee*	dancers
la bambina	*la bambeena*	girl
i bambini	*ee bambeenee*	children
il bambino	*eel bambeeno*	boy
le bambole	*lay bambolay*	dolls
la banana	*la banana*	banana
il banco	*eel banko*	desk
la bandiera	*la bandyaira*	flag
il bar	*eel bar*	café
i barattoli	*ee barattolee*	pots, jars
la barca	*la barka*	boat
la barca a vela	*la barka a vayla*	sailboat
la barca a remi	*la barka a raymee*	rowboat
il baseball	*eel bayzbol*	baseball
basso	*basso*	low
il bastone	*eel bastonay*	stick
i bastoncini da sci	*ee bastoncheenee da shee*	ski poles
la batteria	*la battaireea*	battery
il bebè	*eel bebay*	baby
il becco	*eel bekko*	beak
la benzina	*la bentseena*	gas
bere	*bairay*	to drink
il berretto	*eel bairretto*	cap
il bersaglio	*eel bairsalyo*	target
il bianco	*eel byanko*	white
i bicchieri	*ee beekkyairee*	glasses (for drinking)
la bicicletta	*la beecheekletta*	bicycle
le biglie	*lay beelyay*	marbles
la biglietteria automatica	*la beelyettaireea owtomateeka*	ticket machine
il biglietto di auguri	*eel beelyetto dee owgooree*	birthday card
la bilancia	*la beelancha*	scales
i binari	*ee beenaree*	train track
il biscotto	*eel beeskotto*	cookie
il bisonte	*eel beezontay*	bison
il blu	*eel bloo*	blue
la bocca	*la bokka*	mouth
il bollitore	*eel bolleetoray*	kettle
la borsa	*la borsa*	purse
la borsa della spesa	*la borsa della spayza*	grocery sack
il borsellino	*eel borselleeno*	wallet
la botte	*la bottay*	barrel
le bottiglie	*lay botteelyay*	bottles
i bottoni	*ee bottonee*	buttons
il braccio	*eel bracho*	arm
la brina	*la breena*	frost
il bruco	*eel brooko*	caterpillar

Italian	Pronunciation	English
la buca di sabbia	*la booka dee sabbya*	sandbox
il buco	*eel booko*	hole
le bullette	*lay boolletay*	tacks
i bulloni	*ee boollonee*	bolts
buono	*bwono*	good
il burro	*eel boorro*	butter

C

Italian	Pronunciation	English
il cacciavite	*eel kachaveetay*	screwdriver
cadere	*kadairay*	to fall
il caffè	*eel kaffay*	coffee
il cagnolino	*eel kanyoleeno*	puppy
il calcio	*eel kalcho*	soccer
caldo	*kaldo*	hot
il calendario	*eel kalendaryo*	calendar
la calzamaglia	*la kaltsamalya*	tights
i calzini	*ee kaltseenee*	socks
la camera da letto	*la kamaira da letto*	bedroom
la cameriera	*la kamairyaira*	waitress
il cameriere	*eel kamairyairay*	waiter
la camicia	*la kameecha*	shirt
la camicia da notte	*la kameecha da nottay*	nightgown
il camion	*eel kamyon*	truck
il/la camionista	*la kamyoneesta*	truck driver
camminare	*kammeenaray*	to walk
camminare a carponi	*kammeenaray a karponee*	to crawl
camminare sulla corda	*kammeenaray soolla korda*	to walk a tightrope
la campagna	*la kampanya*	country
il campo	*eel kampo*	field
il campo giochi	*eel kampo jokee*	playground
il canale	*eel kanalay*	canal
il canarino	*eel kanareeno*	canary
la cancellata	*la kanchellata*	railings
il cancello	*eel kanchello*	gate
la candela	*la kandayla*	candle
le candeline	*lay kandeleenay*	cake candles
il cane	*eel kanay*	dog
il cane pastore	*eel kanay pastoray*	sheepdog
il canguro	*eel kangooro*	kangaroo
la canna da pesca	*la kanna da peska*	fishing rod
la cannuccia	*la kannoocha*	straw
la canoa	*la kanoa*	canoe
il canottaggio	*eel kanottajjo*	rowing
la canottiera	*la kanottyaira*	vest
i cantanti	*ee kantantee*	singers
cantare	*kantaray*	to sing
il capannone	*eel kapannonay*	barn
i capelli	*ee kapellee*	hair
il cappello	*eel kappello*	hat
il cappello da sole	*eel kappello da solay*	sun hat
il cappotto	*eel kappotto*	coat
la capra	*la kapra*	goat
la caramella	*la karamella*	candy
il cardigan	*eel kardeegan*	cardigan
la carne	*la karnay*	meat
la carota	*la karota*	carrot
il carrello	*eel karrello*	cart
il carretto	*eel karretto*	cart
la carriola	*la karryola*	wheelbarrow
il carro attrezzi	*eel karro attrettsee*	tow truck
la carrozzina	*la karrottseena*	baby buggy
la carta	*la karta*	paper

Italian	Pronunciation	English
la carta geografica	la **karta** jayogra**fee**ka	map
la carta igienica	la **karta** ee**jen**eeka	toilet paper
la carta vetrata	la **karta** ve**tra**ta	sandpaper
il cartello stradale	eel kar**tell**o stra**da**lay	signpost
le cartoline	lay karto**lee**nay	cards
la casa	la **ka**za	house
la casa colonica	la **ka**za kolo**nee**ka	farmhouse
la casa delle bambole	la **ka**za **dell**ay **bam**bolay	dolls' house
la cascata	la kas**ka**ta	waterfall
il casco	eel **kas**ko	helmet
il casotto	eel ka**zott**o	shed
la cassa	la **kass**a	checkout
la cassetta degli arnesi	la kas**sett**a **del**yee ar**nay**see	tool box
il cassetto	eel kas**sett**o	drawer
il cassettone	eel kasset**ton**ay	chest of drawers
il castello	eel kas**tell**o	castle
il castello di sabbia	eel kas**tell**o dee **sabb**ya	sandcastle
il castoro	eel kas**tor**o	beaver
cattivo	kat**tee**vo	bad
la cavallerizza	la kavallai**reett**sa	bareback rider
il cavalletto	eel kaval**lett**o	easel
il cavallo	eel ka**vall**o	horse
il cavallo a dondolo	eel ka**vall**o a **don**dolo	rocking horse
il cavolfiore	eel kavol**fyor**ay	cauliflower
il cavolo	eel **ka**volo	cabbage
la cena	la **chay**na	supper, dinner
i ceppi	ee **chepp**ee	logs
il cerchio	eel **chair**kyo	circle, hoop
i cereali	ee chaira**yal**ee	cereal
la cerniera lampo	la chair**nyai**ra **lam**po	zipper
il cerotto	eel chai**rott**o	Band-Aid
il cervo	eel **chair**vo	deer
il cespuglio	eel ches**pool**yo	bush
la cesta	la **ches**ta	basket
il cestino	eel ches**tee**no	shopping basket
il cestino della carta	eel ches**tee**no **dell**a **kar**ta	waste paper basket
il cetriolo	eel chetree**ol**o	cucumber
chiaro	**kya**ro	light
la chiatta	la **kyatt**a	barge
la chiave	la **kya**vay	key
la chiave inglese	la **kya**vay een**glay**zay	wrench
la chiocciola	la **kyo**chola	snail
i chiodi	ee **kyo**dee	nails
la chitarra	la kee**tarr**a	guitar
la chiusa	la **kyoo**za	lock (canal)
chiuso	**kyoo**zo	closed
il cibo in scatola	eel **chee**bo een **ska**tola	canned food
il cibo	eel **chee**bo	food
il ciclismo	eel chee**kleez**mo	cycling
il cielo	eel **chay**lo	sky
i cigni	ee **chee**nyee	swans
la ciliegia	la chee**lye**ja	cherry
il cilindro	eel chee**leen**dro	top hat
il cinema	eel **chee**nayma	movie theater
cinque	**cheen**quay	five
la cintura	la cheen**too**ra	belt
la cioccolata	la **chokk**olata	chocolate
la cioccolata calda	la **chokk**olata **kal**da	hot chocolate
i ciottoli	ee **chott**olee	pebbles
la cipolla	la chee**poll**a	onion
il circo	eel **cheer**ko	circus
la coccinella	la kochee**nell**a	ladybug
il coccodrillo	eel kokko**dreell**o	crocodile
la coda	la **ko**da	tail
il cofano	eel **ko**fano	hood (of a car)
la colazione	la kolat**syo**nay	breakfast
la colla	la **koll**a	glue
la collana	la **koll**ana	necklace
la collina	la **koll**eena	hill
il collo	eel **koll**o	neck
i colori	ee ko**lor**ee	colors, paints
i colori per il viso	ee ko**lor**ee pair eel **vee**zo	face paints
i coltelli	ee kol**tell**ee	knives
il comignolo	eel ko**mee**nyolo	chimney
il Compact Disc	eel **kom**pat deesk	CD
il compleanno	eel komplay**ann**o	birthday
comprare	kompra**ray**	to buy
il computer	eel kom**pyoo**tair	computer
la conchiglia	la kon**kee**lya	shell
il conducente di autobus	eel kondoo**chen**tay dee **owt**oboos	bus driver
le condutture	lay kondoot**too**ray	pipes
il coniglio	eel ko**nee**lyo	rabbit
il cono	eel **ko**no	cone
i contrari	ee kon**trar**ee	opposites
il controllore	eel kontrol**lor**ay	ticket inspector
la corda per saltare	la **kor**da pair sal**tar**ay	jump-rope
le corna	lay **kor**na	horns
correre	**korr**airay	to run
la corsa campestre	la **kor**sa kam**pes**tray	running race
corto	**kor**to	short
le costruzioni	lay kostroot**syo**nee	building blocks
il costume da bagno	eel kos**too**may da **ban**yo	swimsuit
i costumi	ee kos**too**mee	costume
il cotone idrofilo	eel ko**ton**ay eedro**feel**o	cotton balls
la cravatta	la kra**vatt**a	tie
il criceto	eel kree**chay**to	hamster
il cricket	eel **kree**ket	cricket
il cubo	eel **koo**bo	cube
i cucchiaini	ee kookkya-**een**ee	teaspoons
la cuccia	la **koo**cha	kennel
la cucina	la koo**chee**na	kitchen
cucinare	koochee**nar**ay	to cook
cucire	koo**chee**ray	to sew
il cugino	eel koo**jee**no	cousin
il cuoco	eel **kwo**ko	cook
il cuscino	eel koo**shee**no	cushion

D

Italian	Pronunciation	English
i dadi (da officina)	ee **da**dee (da offee**chee**na)	nuts (workshop)
i dadi (per giocare)	ee **da**dee (pair jo**kar**ay)	dice
la damigella d'onore	la damee**jell**a do**nor**ay	bridesmaid
la danza	la **dant**sa	dancing
davanti	da**van**tee	front
le decorazioni di carta	lay dekorat**syo**nee dee **kar**ta	paper chains
il delfino	eel del**fee**no	dolphin
i denti	ee **den**tee	teeth
il dentifricio	eel dentee**free**cho	toothpaste
il/la dentista	eel/la den**tees**ta	dentist
dentro	**den**tro	inside
destra	**des**tra	right
il detersivo	eel detair**see**vo	laundry detergent
diciannove	deechan**nov**ay	nineteen
diciassette	deechas**sett**ay	seventeen
diciotto	dee**chott**o	eighteen
dieci	**dye**chee	ten
dietro	**dye**tro	behind
difficile	deef**fee**cheelay	difficult
dipingere	deepeen**jai**ray	to paint

il disegno	*eel dee**sen**yo*	drawing
il distributore di benzina	*eel deestreeboo**tor**ay dee bent**seen**a*	gas pump
le dita dei piedi	*lay **dee**ta day **pye**dee*	toes
le dita della mano	*lay **dee**ta **del**la **man**o*	fingers
il divano	*eel dee**van**o*	sofa
la doccia	*la **doch**a*	shower
dodici	***do**deechee*	twelve
i dolci	*ee **dol**chee*	dessert
il domatore	*eel doma**tor**ay*	ringmaster
domenica	*dome**neek**a*	Sunday
la donna	*la **donn**a*	woman
dormire	*dor**meer**ay*	to sleep
il dottore	*eel dot**tor**ay*	doctor
la dottoressa	*la dotto**ress**a*	(woman) doctor
il dromedario	*eel dromed**ar**yo*	camel
due	***doo**ay*	two
duro	***doo**ro*	hard

E

l'elefante (m)	*lele**fan**tay*	elephant
l'elicottero (m)	*lelee**kott**airo*	helicopter
l'equilibrista (m)	*lekweelee**brees**ta*	tightrope walker
l'equitazione (f)	*lekweeta**tsyon**ay*	riding
l'erba (f)	***lairb**a*	grass
l'esca (f)	***lesk**a*	bait
l'estate (m)	*les**tat**ay*	summer

F

la fabbrica	*la **fabb**reeka*	factory
facile	***fach**eelay*	easy
i fagiolini	*ee fajo**leen**ee*	beans
la falce di luna	*la **fal**chay dee **loon**a*	crescent
il falegname	*eel falen**yam**ay*	carpenter
la falena	*la fa**layn**a*	moth
il falò	*eel fa**lo***	bonfire
la famiglia	*la fa**meel**ya*	family
il fango	*eel **fang**o*	mud
fare	***far**ay*	to make, to do
fare a botte	***far**ay a **bott**ay*	to fight
la farfalla	*la far**fall**a*	butterfly
il farfallino	*eel farfal**leen**o*	bow tie
la farina	*la fa**reen**a*	flour
il faro	*eel **far**o*	lighthouse
la fascia	*la **fash**a*	bandage
la fattoria	*la fatto**ree**a*	farm
i fazzoletti di carta	*ee fatt**solet**tee dee **kart**a*	tissues
il fazzoletto	*eel fatt**solet**to*	handkerchief
la felpa	*la **felp**a*	sweatshirt
il ferro da stiro	*eel **fairr**o da **steer**o*	iron
la festa	*la **fest**a*	party
i fiammiferi	*ee fyam**mee**fairee*	matches
la fibbia	*la **feebb**ya*	buckle
il fienile	*eel fye**neel**ay*	hay loft
il fieno	*eel **fyen**o*	hay
la figlia	*la **feel**ya*	daughter
il figlio	*eel **feel**yo*	son
la finestra	*la fee**nest**ra*	window
i fiori	*ee **fyor**ee*	flowers
il fischietto	*eel fees**kyet**to*	whistle
il fiume	*eel **fyoo**may*	river
il flauto dolce	*eel **flow**to **dol**chay*	recorder
la foca	*la **fok**a*	seal
le foglie	*lay **fol**yay*	leaves

il football americano	*eel **foot**bol amaireek**an**o*	football
le forbici	*lay **for**beechee*	scissors
le forchette	*lay for**ket**tay*	forks
il forcone	*eel for**kon**ay*	rake
la foresta	*la for**est**a*	forest
il formaggio	*eel for**majj**o*	cheese
le forme	*lay **for**may*	shapes
il fornaio	*eel for**na**-yo*	baker (man)
la fornaia	*la for**na**-ya*	baker (woman)
la foschia	*la **fosk**ya*	mist
le fotografie	*lay fotogra**fee**-ay*	photos
il fotografo	*eel fo**tog**rafo*	photographer
la fragola	*la **frag**ola*	strawberry
il fratello	*eel fra**tell**o*	brother
le frecce	*lay **frech**ay*	arrows
freddo	***fredd**o*	cold
il frigorifero	*eel freego**ree**fairo*	fridge
la frittata	*la freet**tat**a*	omelette
le frittelle	*lay freet**tell**ay*	pancakes
la frutta	*la **froott**a*	fruit
il frutteto	*eel froot**tay**to*	orchard
il fucile	*eel foo**chee**lay*	gun
il fumetto	*eel foo**mett**o*	comic
il fumo	*eel **foo**mo*	smoke
il funambolo	*eel foo**nam**bolo*	tightrope walker
la fune	*la **foon**ay*	rope
il fungo	*eel **foong**o*	mushroom
i fuochi d'artificio	*ee **fwok**ee dartee**fee**cho*	fireworks
fuori	***fwor**ee*	outside
il furgone	*eel foor**gon**ay*	van

G

la gabbia	*la **gabb**ya*	cage
il gabbiano	*eel gabb**yan**o*	seagull
la galleria	*la gallai**ree**a*	tunnel
le galline	*lay gal**leen**ay*	hens
il gallo	*eel **gall**o*	rooster
la gamba	*la **gamb**a*	leg
il gattino	*eel gat**teen**o*	kitten
il gatto	*eel **gatt**o*	cat
il gelato	*eel je**lat**o*	ice cream
i gessetti	*ee jes**sett**ee*	chalks
il gesso	*eel **jess**o*	cast
il giallo	*eel **jall**o*	yellow
il giardino	*eel jar**deen**o*	yard
la ginnastica artistica	*la jeen**nas**teeka artees**teek**a*	gymnastics
il ginocchio	*eel jee**nokk**yo*	knee
giocare	*jo**kar**ay*	to play
i giocattoli	*ee jo**katt**olee*	toys
il giocoliere	*eel joko**lyair**ay*	juggler
il giornale	*eel jor**nal**ay*	newspaper
i giorni	*ee **jor**nee*	days
i giorni speciali	*ee **jor**nee spe**chal**ee*	special days
la giostra	*la **jost**ra*	merry-go-round
giovedì	*jove**dee***	Thursday
la giraffa	*la jee**raff**a*	giraffe
i girini	*ee jee**reen**ee*	tadpoles
giù	*joo*	down
il giubbotto	*eel joob**bott**o*	jacket
il giudice	*eel **joo**deechay*	judge
il gomito	*eel **gom**eeto*	elbow
la gomma	*la **gomm**a*	eraser
la gonna	*la **gonn**a*	skirt
il gorilla	*eel go**reell**a*	gorilla
il granchio	*eel **grank**yo*	crab

Italian	Pronunciation	English
grande	*gran*day	big
grasso	*grasso*	fat
il grembiule	eel gremb*byoo*lay	apron
il grigio	eel *gree*jo	gray
la gru	la *groo*	crane
le grucce	lay *groo*chay	crutches
la guancia	la *gwan*cha	cheek
il guanciale	eel gwan*cha*lay	pillow
i guanti	ee *gwan*tee	gloves
guardare	gwar*da*ray	to look
il guinzaglio	eel gween*tsal*yo	lead
il gufo	eel *goo*fo	owl

H

Italian	Pronunciation	English
l'hamburger (m)	*lam*boorgair	hamburger
l'hostess (f)	*lo*stess	flight attendant

I

Italian	Pronunciation	English
l'iceberg (m)	*lies*bairg	iceberg
l'imbianchino (m)	leembyan*kee*no	house painter
in cima	een *chee*ma	on top
in fondo	een *fon*do	at the bottom
l'infermiere (m)	leenfair*myair*ay	nurse (man)
l'infermiera (f)	leenfair*myair*a	nurse (woman)
l'ingresso (m)	leen*gres*so	hall
l'insalata (f)	leensa*la*ta	salad
l'insegnante (m/f)	leense*nyan*tay	teacher
l'interruttore (m)	leentairroot*tor*ay	switch
l'inverno (m)	leen*vair*no	winter
l'ippopotamo (m)	leeppo*po*tamo	hippopotamus
l'isola (f)	*lee*zola	island

J

Italian	Pronunciation	English
i jeans	ee jeens	jeans
il jogging	eel *jog*geeng	jogging
il judo	eel *joo*do	judo

K

Italian	Pronunciation	English
il karatè	eel kara*tay*	karate
il ketchup	eel *ke*chap	ketchup

L

Italian	Pronunciation	English
le labbra	lay *labb*ra	lips
il laboratorio	eel labora*tor*yo	workshop
i lacci per le scarpe	ee *la*chee pair lay *skar*pay	shoelaces
il lago	eel *la*go	lake
la lampada	la *lam*pada	lamp
la lampadina	la lampa*dee*na	light bulb
il lampione	eel lam*pyon*ay	street lamp
il lampo	eel *lam*po	lightning
il lampone	eel lam*pon*ay	raspberry

Italian	Pronunciation	English
lanciare	lan*char*ay	to throw
il latte	eel *lat*tay	milk
la lattuga	la lat*too*ga	lettuce
la lavagna	la la*van*ya	board
il lavandino	eel lavan*dee*no	sink
lavarsi	la*var*see	to wash
la lavatrice	la lava*tree*chay	washing machine
il lavello	eel la*vel*lo	sink
lavorare a maglia	lavo*rar*ay a *mal*ya	to knit
leggere	*lejj*airay	to read
il legno	eel *len*yo	wood
lento	*len*to	slow
il lenzuolo	eel len*tswo*lo	sheet
i leoncini	ee layon*chee*nee	lion cubs
il leone	eel la*yon*ay	lion
il leopardo	eel layo*par*do	leopard
le lettere	lay *lett*airay	letters
il letto	eel *let*to	bed
i libri	ee *lee*bree	books
la lima	la *lee*ma	file
il limone	eel lee*mon*ay	lemon
la lingua	la *leen*gwa	tongue
il locomotore	eel loko*mo*toray	engine (train)
lontano	lon*ta*no	far
la lucertola	la loo*chair*tola	lizard
la luna	la *loo*na	moon
il luna park	eel *loo*na park	amusement park
lunedì	loonay*dee*	Monday
lungo	*loon*go	long
il lupo	eel *loo*po	wolf

M

Italian	Pronunciation	English
la macchina	la *ma*keena	car
la macchina da corsa	la *ma*keena da *kor*sa	racing car
la macchina della polizia	la *ma*keena *del*la polee*tsee*a	police car
la macchina fotografica	la *mak*keena foto*gra*feeka	camera
il macchinista	eel makkee*nee*sta	conductor
il macellaio	eel machel*la*-yo	butcher
la madre	la *ma*dray	mother
la maglietta	la mal*yet*ta	tee-shirt
il maglione	eel mal*yon*ay	sweater
magro	*ma*gro	thin
i maiali	ee ma-*ya*lee	pigs
i maialini	ee ma-ya*lee*nee	piglets
il mandarino	eel manda*ree*no	tangerine
mangiare	man*jar*ay	to eat
la maniglia della porta	la ma*neel*ya *del*la *por*ta	door handle
la mano	la *ma*no	hand
il mappamondo	eel mappa*mon*do	globe
il marciapiede	eel marcha*pye*day	sidewalk
il mare	eel *mar*ay	sea
il marinaio	eel maree*na*-yo	sailor
le marionette	lay maryo*net*tay	puppets
il marito	eel ma*ree*to	husband
la marmellata	la marmel*la*ta	jelly
il marrone	eel mar*ron*ay	brown
martedì	marte*dee*	Tuesday
il martello	eel mar*tel*lo	hammer
il martello pneumatico	eel mar*tel*lo pnayoo*ma*teeko	drill
le maschere	lay *ma*skairay	masks
i massi	ee *ma*ssee	rocks
la matita	la ma*tee*ta	pencil

Italian	Pronunciation	English
il matrimonio	eel matreemonyo	wedding
la mattina	la matteena	morning
le mattonelle	lay mattonellay	tiles
i mattoni	ee mattonee	bricks
la mazza	la mattsa	bat (sports)
me stesso	may stesso	myself
i meccanici	ee mekkaneechee	mechanics
la medicina	la medeecheena	medicine
la mela	la mayla	apple
il melone	eel maylonay	melon
il mento	eel mento	chin
il mercato	eel mairkato	market
mercoledì	mairkolaydee	Wednesday
i mestieri	ee mestyairee	jobs
i mestoli	ee mestolee	wooden spoons
il metro	eel metro	tape measure
il miele	eel myelay	honey
la minestra	la meenestra	soup
la moglie	la molyay	wife
molti	moltee	many
la mongolfiera	la mongolfyaira	hot air balloon
la montagna	la montanya	mountain
le montagne russe	lay montanyay roossay	rollercoaster
la moquette	la mokett	carpet
morbido	morbeedo	soft
la morsa	la morsa	vise
morto	morto	dead
la mosca	la moska	fly
la motocicletta	la motocheekletta	motorcycle
il motore	eel motoray	engine (car)
il motoscafo	eel motoskafo	motor boat
la mucca	la mookka	cow
il mucchio di fieno	eel mookkyo dee fyeno	haystack
il mulino a vento	eel mooleeno a vento	windmill
la musicassetta	la moozeekassetta	cassette
le mutande	lay mootanday	underwear

N

Italian	Pronunciation	English
nascondersi	naskondairsee	to hide
il naso	eel nazo	nose
il nastro	eel nastro	ribbon
Natale	natalay	Christmas
la nave	la navay	ship
la nebbia	la nebbya	fog
il negozio	eel negotsyo	shop
il nero	eel nairo	black
la neve	la nayvay	snow
il nido	eel needo	nest
la nonna	la nonna	grandmother
il nonno	eel nonno	grandfather
la notte	la nottay	night
nove	novay	nine
i numeri	ee noomairee	numbers
il nuoto	eel nwoto	swimming
nuovo	nwovo	new
le nuvole	lay noovolay	clouds

O

Italian	Pronunciation	English
l'occhio (m)	lokkyo	eye
le oche	lay okay	geese
l'olio (m)	lolyo	oil
l'ombrello (m)	lombrello	umbrella
l'ombrellone (m)	lombrellonay	beach umbrella
le onde	lay onday	waves

Italian	Pronunciation	English
l'orchestra (f)	lorkestra	orchestra
le orecchie	lay orekkyay	ears
l'orologio (m)	lorolojo	clock, watch
l'orsacchiotto (m)	lorsakkyotto	teddy bear
l'orso (m)	lorso	bear
l'orso (m) polare	lorso polaray	polar bear
l'ospedale (m)	lospedalay	hospital
l'osso (m)	losso	bone
otto	otto	eight
l'ovale (m)	lovalay	oval

P

Italian	Pronunciation	English
la padella	la padella	frying pan
il padre	eel padray	father
la pagaia	la paga-ya	paddle
il pagliaccio	eel palyacho	clown
il palazzo	eel palattso	block of apartments, building
la paletta (da giardino)	la paletta (da jardeeno)	shovel
la paletta (da spiaggia)	la paletta (da spyajja)	beach shovel
la paletta (per la spazzatura)	la paletta (pair la spattsatoora)	dustpan
la palla	la palla	ball
la pallacanestro	la pallakanestro	basketball
il palloncino	eel palloncheeno	balloon
la panchina	la pankeena	bench
la pancia	la pancha	tummy
il panda	eel panda	panda
il pane	eel panay	bread
il pane tostato	eel panay tostato	toast
il panino	eel paneeno	sandwich
la panna	la panna	cream
il pannolino	eel pannoleeno	diaper
i pantaloncini	ee pantaloncheenee	shorts
i pantaloni	ee pantalonee	pants
le pantofole	lay pantofolay	slippers
il pappagallino	eel pappagalleeno	parakeet
il pappagallo	eel pappagallo	parrot
il paracadute	eel parakadootay	parachute
il parco	eel parko	park
la parete	la paraytay	wall
parlare	parlaray	to talk
il parrucchiere	eel parrookkyairay	hairdresser
il passeggino	eel passejjeeno	stroler
i pastelli	ee pastellee	crayons
i pasti	ee pastee	meals
la pastorella	la pastorella	shepherdess
le patate	lay patatay	potatoes
le patatine	lay patateenay	chips
le patatine fritte	lay patateenay freettay	French fries
il pattinaggio su ghiaccio	eel patteenajjio soo gyacho	ice skating
i pattini	ee patteenee	skates
la pattumiera	la pattoomyaira	trash can
il pavimento	eel paveemento	floor
le pecore	lay paykoray	sheep
il pellicano	eel pelleekano	pelican
la penna	la penna	pen
i pennarelli	ee pennarellee	felt-tips
il pennello	eel pennello	paintbrush
pensare	pensaray	to think
la pensilina	la penseeleena	platform
le pentole	le pentolay	pans

Italian	Pronunciation	English
il pepe	eel *paypay*	pepper
la pera	la *paira*	pear
le perline	lay *pairleenay*	beads
la pesca (frutto)	la *peska (frootto)*	peach
la pesca (attività)	la *peska (atteeveeta)*	fishing
il pescatore	eel *peskatoray*	fisherman
il pesce	eel *peshay*	fish
il peschereccio	eel *peskairecho*	fishing boat
i pesci rossi	ee *peshee rossee*	goldfish
la petroliera	la *petrolyaira*	oil tanker
il pettine	eel *petteenay*	comb
la pialla	la *pyalla*	plane (shaving)
il pianeta	eel *pyanayta*	planet
piangere	*pyanjairay*	to cry
il piano di lavoro	eel *pyano dee lavoro*	workbench
il pianoforte	eel *pyanofortay*	piano
la pianta	la *pyanta*	plant
i piatti	ee *pyattee*	plates
i piattini	ee *pyatteenee*	saucers
il piccione	eel *peechonay*	pigeon
piccolo	*peekkolo*	small
il picnic	eel *peekneek*	picnic
il piede	eel *pyeday*	foot
pieno	*pyeno*	full
le pietre	lay *pyetray*	stones
il pigiama	eel *peejama*	pajamas
le pillole	lay *peellolay*	pills
il pilota	eel *peelota*	pilot
il ping-pong	eel *peeng-pong*	ping-pong
il pinguino	eel *peengweeno*	penguin
le pinne	lay *peennay*	flippers
la pioggia	la *pyojja*	rain
il pipistrello	eel *peepeestrello*	bat (animal)
la piscina	la *peesheena*	swimming poo
i piselli	ee *peezellee*	peas
la pista di atterraggio	la *peesta dee attairrajjo*	runway
le piume	lay *pyoomay*	feathers
il piumone	eel *pyoomonay*	comforter
la pizza	la *peettsa*	pizza
la plastilina	la *plasteeleena*	modeling doug
il pneumatico	lo *pnayoomateeko*	tire
pochi	*pokee*	few
i poliziotti	ee *poleetsyottee*	policemen
il pollaio	eel *polla-yo*	hen-house
il pollice	eel *polleechay*	thumb
il pollo	eel *pollo*	chicken
il pomodoro	eel *pomodoro*	tomato
il pompelmo	eel *pompelmo*	grapefruit
il pompiere	eel *pompyairay*	fireman
il ponte	eel *pontay*	bridge
il pony	eel *ponee*	pony
il pop-corn	eel *pop-korn*	popcorn
il porcellino d'India	eel *porchelleeno deendya*	guinea pig
il porcile	eel *porcheelay*	pigsty
il porro	eel *porro*	leek
la porta	la *porta*	door
il portabagagli	eel *portabagalyee*	trunk (of car)
portare	*portaray*	to carry
i poster	ee *postair*	posters
il postino	eel *posteeno*	postman
la pozzanghera	la *pottsangaira*	puddle
il pranzo	eel *prantso*	lunch, dinner
prendere	*prendairay*	to take
la primavera	la *preemavaira*	spring
primo	*preemo*	first
la proboscide	la *probosheeday*	trunk
il prosciutto	eel *proshootto*	ham
i pulcini	ee *poolcheenee*	chickens
pulito	*pooleeto*	clean
le puntine da disegno	lay *poonteenay da deesenyo*	thumb tacks
il purè	eel *pooray*	mashed potato
il puzzle	eel *pazol*	puzzle

Q

Italian	Pronunciation	English
il quaderno	eel *kwadairno*	notebook
il quadrato	eel *kwadrato*	square
quattordici	*kwattordeechee*	fourteen
quattro	*kwattro*	four
quindici	*kweendeechee*	fifteen

R

Italian	Pronunciation	English
la racchetta	la *rakketta*	racket
raccogliere	*rakkolyairay*	to pick
il radiatore	eel *radyatoray*	radiator
la radio	la *radyo*	radio
la ragnatela	la *ranyatayla*	spider's web
il ragno	eel *ranyo*	spider
i ramoscelli	ee *ramoshellee*	twigs
la rana	la *rana*	frog
il rastrello	eel *rastrello*	rake
il razzo	eel *rattso*	rocket
il regalo	eel *regalo*	present
il remo	eel *remo*	oar
la renna	la *renna*	reindeer
i respingenti	ee *respeenjentee*	buffers
la rete	la *raytay*	net
la rete di sicurezza	la *raytay dee seekoorettsa*	safety net
il rettangolo	eel *rettangolo*	rectangle
il riccio	eel *reecho*	hedgehog
ridere	*reedairay*	to laugh
il righello	eel *reegello*	ruler
il rimorchio	eel *reemorkyo*	trailer
il rinoceronte	eel *reenochairontay*	rhinoceros
il riso	eel *reezo*	rice
il robot	eel *robot*	robot
i rollerblades	ee *rollerblades*	rollerblades
il rombo	eel *rombo*	diamond (shape)
rompere	*rompairay*	to break
il rosa	eel *roza*	pink
il rospo	eel *rospo*	toad
il rosso	eel *rosso*	red
la roulotte	la *roolott*	caravan
il rubinetto	eel *roobeenetto*	tap
il rugby	eel *ragbee*	rugby
la rugiada	la *roojada*	dew
la ruota	la *rwota*	wheel, big wheel
il ruscello	eel *rooshello*	stream

S

Italian	Pronunciation	English
sabato	*sabato*	Saturday
la sala d'aspetto	la *sala daspetto*	waiting room
il salame	eel *salamay*	salami
il sale	eel *salay*	salt
la salsiccia	la *salseecha*	sausage
saltare	*saltaray*	to jump
saltare la corda	*saltaray la korda*	to skip
il salvadanaio	eel *salvadana-yo*	money box

Italian	Pronunciation	English
i sandali	ee **sand**alee	sandals
il sapone	eel sa**po**nay	soap
la scala	la **ska**la	ladder
la scala di corda	la **ska**la dee **kor**da	rope ladder
le scale	lay **ska**lay	stairs
gli scalini	lyee ska**lee**nee	steps
le scarpe	lay **skar**pay	shoes
le scarpe da ginnastica	lay **skar**pay da jeen**nas**teeka	tennis shoes
la scatola	la **ska**tola	box, can
scavare	ska**va**ray	to dig
la scavatrice	la skava**tree**chay	bulldozer
lo schiacciasassi	lo skyacha**sas**see	roller
la schiena	la **sky**ena	back
gli sci	lyee shee	skis
lo sci	lo shee	skiing
lo sci nautico	lo shee **now**teeko	waterskiing
la sciarpa	la **shar**pa	scarf
la scimmia	la **sheem**mya	monkey
lo scivolo	lo **shee**volo	slide
le scodelle	lay sko**del**lay	bowls
la scogliera	la sko**lyai**ra	cliff
lo scoiattolo	lo sko**yat**tolo	squirrel
la scopa	la **sko**pa	broom
scrivere	**skree**vairay	to write
la scuderia	la skoo**dai**reea	stable
la scuola	la **skwo**la	school
scuro	**skoo**ro	dark
il secchiello	eel sek**kyel**lo	bucket
il sedano	eel **se**dano	celery
il sedere	eel se**dai**ray	bottom
la sedia	la **se**dya	chair
la sedia a rotelle	la **se**dya a ro**tel**lay	wheelchair
la sedia a sdraio	la **se**dya a **zdra**-yo	deckchair
sedici	**say**deechee	sixteen
la sega	la **say**ga	saw
la segatura	la sayga**too**ra	sawdust
la seggiovia	la sejjo**vee**a	chairlift
i segnali	ee sen**ya**lee	signals
sei	say	six
la sella	la **sel**la	saddle
il semaforo	eel se**ma**foro	traffic lights
i semi	ee **say**mee	seeds
il sentiero	eel sen**tyai**ro	path
la sera	la **sai**ra	evening
il serpente	eel sair**pen**tay	snake
la serra	la **sair**ra	greenhouse
sette	**set**tay	seven
lo sgabello	lo zga**bel**lo	stool
la siepe	la **sye**pay	hedge
sinistra	see**nee**stra	left
la siringa	la see**reen**ga	syringe
lo skateboard	lo **sket**bord	skateboard
la slitta	la **sleet**ta	sleigh
lo snowboard	lo **sno**bord	snowboard
soffiare	soff**ya**ray	to blow
il soffitto	eel sof**feet**to	ceiling
il soggiorno	eel soj**jor**no	living room
i soldatini	ee solda**tee**nee	toy soldiers
i soldi	ee **sol**dee	money
il sole	eel **so**lay	sun
sopra	**so**pra	above
le sopracciglia	lay sopra**chee**lya	eyebrows
la sorella	la so**rel**la	sister
sorridere	sor**ree**dairay	to smile
sotto	**sot**to	below
il sottomarino	eel sotto**ma**reeno	submarine
spaccare	spak**ka**ray	to chop
gli spaghetti	lyee spa**get**tee	spaghetti
lo spago	lo **spa**go	string
le spalle	lay **spal**lay	shoulders
lo spaventapasseri	lo spaventa**pas**sairee	scarecrow
lo Spazio	lo **spa**tsyo	space
spazzare	spat**tsa**ray	to sweep
la spazzatura	la spattsa**too**ra	trash
la spazzola	la **spatt**sola	brush, hairbrush
lo spazzolino	lo spattso**lee**no	toothbrush
lo spazzolone	lo spattso**lo**nay	mop
lo specchio	lo **spek**kyo	mirror
la spiaggia	la **spyaj**ja	beach
la spilla	la **speel**la	badge
gli spinaci	lyee spee**na**chee	spinach
spingere	**speen**jairay	to push
lo spogliatoio	lo spolya**to**yo	changing room
sporco	**spor**ko	dirty
lo sport	lo sport	sport
la sposa	la **spo**za	bride
lo sposo	lo **spo**zo	bridegroom
la spugna	la **spoon**ya	sponge
lo squalo	lo **skwa**lo	shark
la staccionata	la stacho**na**ta	fence
le stagioni	lay sta**jo**nee	seasons
lo stagno	lo **stan**yo	pond
la stalla	la **stal**la	cowshed
stare seduti	**sta**ray se**doo**tee	to sit
la stazione di servizio	la stat**syo**nay dee sair**veet**syo	service station
la stazione ferroviaria	la stat**syo**nay fairrov**yar**ya	station
la stella	la **stel**la	star
la stella marina	la **stel**la ma**ree**na	starfish
lo steward	lo **styoo**ward	flight attendant
gli stivali di gomma	lyee stee**va**lee dee **gom**ma	boots
lo straccio	lo **stra**cho	duster
la strada	la **stra**da	street
le strisce pedonali	lay **stree**shay pedo**na**lee	pedestrian crossin
lo struzzo	lo **stroot**tso	ostrich
su	soo	up
il subacqueo	eel soobak**kwa**yo	diver
il succo di frutta	eel **sook**ko dee **froot**ta	fruit juice
il sumo	eel **soo**mo	sumo wrestling
la susina	la soo**zee**na	plum

T

Italian	Pronunciation	English
i tacchini	ee tak**kee**nee	turkeys
tagliare	ta**lya**ray	to cut
la talpa	la **tal**pa	mole
i tamburi	ee tam**boo**ree	drums
il tappetino	eel tappay**tee**no	rug
il tappeto	eel tap**pay**to	carpet
la tartaruga	la tarta**roo**ga	tortoise
le tasche	lay **tas**kay	pockets
il tasso	eel **tas**so	badger
il tavolino	eel tavo**lee**no	small table
il taxi	eel **tak**see	taxi
le tazze	lay **tatt**say	cups
il tè	eel tay	tea
la teiera	la ta**yai**ra	teapot
il telefono	eel te**le**fono	telephone
il telescopio	eel teles**kop**yo	telescope
il televisore	eel televee**zo**ray	television
il temperino	eel tempe**ree**no	pocketknife
il tempo	eel **tem**po	weather
la tenda	la **ten**da	curtain, tent
le tende	lay **ten**day	curtains, tents

Italian	Pronunciation	English
il tennis	eel **tennees**	tennis
il termometro	eel **tair**mo**maytro**	thermometer
la terra	la **tairra**	earth
la testa	la **testa**	head
il tetto	eel **tetto**	roof
la tigre	la **tee**gray	tiger
tirare	teer**a**ray	to pull
il tiro a segno	eel **teero** a **senyo**	rifle range
il tiro al cerchietto	eel **teero** al chair**kyetto**	ring toss
il tiro con l'arco	eel **teero** kon **larko**	archery
il topolino	eel topo**leeno**	mouse
il torace	eel tor**a**chay	chest
il toro	eel **toro**	bull
la torre di controllo	la **torray** dee kon**trollo**	control tower
la torta	la **torta**	cake, birthday cake
il tosaerba	eel toza-**airba**	lawnmower
la tovaglia	la to**valya**	tablecloth
il trapano	eel **trapano**	drill
il trapezio	eel tra**pet**syo	trapeze
i trasporti	ee tras**por**tee	transportation
il trattore	eel trat**toray**	tractor
tre	tray	three
tredici	**tray**deechee	thirteen
il trenino	eel tray**neeno**	toy train
il trenino dei fantasmi	eel tray**neeno** day fant**az**mee	ghost train
il treno	eel **trayno**	train
il treno merci	eel **trayno mair**chee	goods train
il triangolo	eel tree**angolo**	triangle
il triciclo	eel tree**cheeklo**	tricycle
la tromba	la **tromba**	trumpet
i trucioli	ee **troo**chyolee	shavings
il tubo di gomma	eel **toobo** dee **gomma**	hosepipe
i tuffi	ee **tooffee**	diving

U

Italian	Pronunciation	English
gli uccelli	lyee oo**chellee**	birds
ultimo	**oolteemo**	last
undici	**oondeechee**	eleven
uno	**oono**	one
l'uomo (m)	**lwomo**	man
le uova	lay **wova**	eggs
l'uovo (m) fritto	**lwovo freetto**	fried egg
l'uovo (m) sodo	**lwovo** sodo	hard-boiled egg
l'uva	**loova**	grapes

V

Italian	Pronunciation	English
la vacanza	la va**kantsa**	vacation
i vagoni	ee va**gonee**	carriages
la valigia	la va**leeja**	suitcase
la vanga	la **vanga**	spade
la vasca	la **vaska**	bathtub
il vassoio	eel vas**soyo**	tray
vecchio	**vekkyo**	old
la vela	la **vayla**	sailing
veloce	vay**lochay**	fast
venerdì	venair**dee**	Friday
venti	**ventee**	twenty
il vento	eel **vento**	wind
il verde	eel **vairday**	green
la verdura	la vair**doora**	vegetables
il verme	eel **vairmay**	worm
la vernice	la vair**neechay**	paint
la vespa	la **vespa**	wasp

Italian	Pronunciation	English
la vestaglia	la ves**talya**	bathrobe
i vestiti	ee ves**teetee**	clothes
il vestito	eel ves**teeto**	dress
il veterinario	eel vetairee**naryo**	vet
vicino	vee**cheeno**	near
la videocassetta	la veedayo**kassetta**	video
il vigile urbano	eel **vee**jeelay oor**bano**	policeman (traffic police)
il villaggio	eel veel**lajjo**	village
il viola	eel **vyola**	purple
il viso	eel **veezo**	face
il vitello	eel vee**tello**	calf
le viti	lay **veetee**	screws
vivo	**veevo**	alive
il volo libero	eel **volo lee**bairo	hang gliding
i volpacchiotti	ee volpak**kyottee**	fox cubs
la volpe	la **volpay**	fox
vuoto	**vwoto**	empty

W

Italian	Pronunciation	English
il water	eel **vatair**	toilet
il windsurf	eel **ween**sairf	windsurfing

Y

Italian	Pronunciation	English
lo yogurt	lo **yo**goort	yogurt

Z

Italian	Pronunciation	English
lo zaino	lo **tsa**-eeno	backpack
le zampe	lay **tsam**pay	paws
la zappa	la **tsappa**	hoe
la zebra	la **tsebra**	zebra
la zia	la **tseea**	aunt
lo zio	lo **tseeo**	uncle
lo zoo	lo **tsoo**	zoo
la zucca	la **tsookka**	pumpkin
lo zucchero	lo **tsookkairo**	sugar
lo zucchero filato	lo **tsookkairo** fee**lato**	cotton candy

This revised edition first published in 1999 by Usborne Publishing Ltd, Usborne House, 83-85 Saffron Hill, London EC1N 8RT, England. www.usborne.com
Based on a previous title first published in 1983.
Copyright © 2002, 1999, 1995, 1983, 1979 Usborne Publishing Ltd. AE. First published in America in 2000. This edition published in 2003.